# STRENGTH AND STONE

THE KINGDOMS OF CHARTILE

# STRENGTH AND STONE

— A PROPHECY COMPANION —

## CASSANDRA MORGAN

WHITE WHISKER PUBLICATIONS

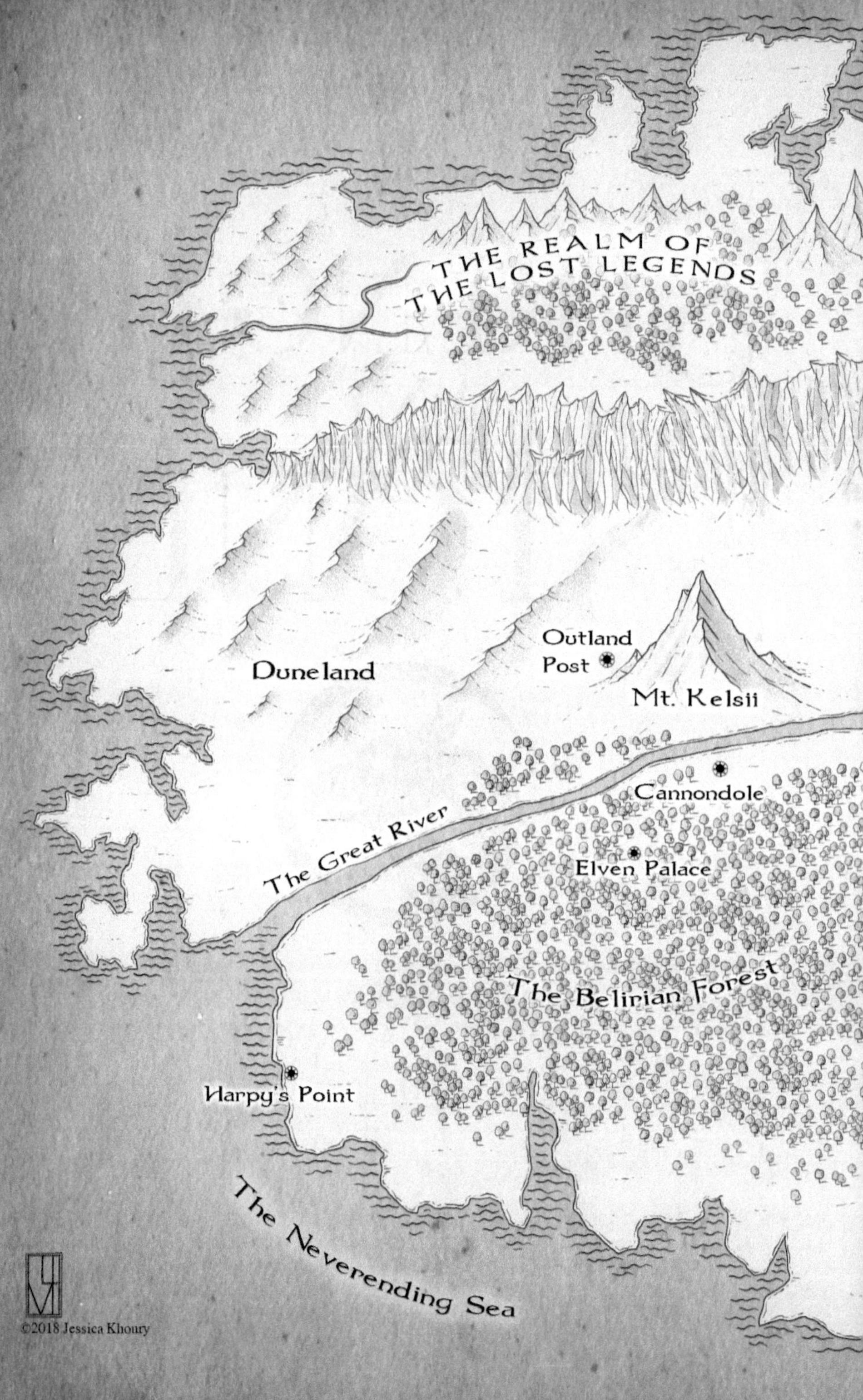
THE REALM OF
THE LOST LEGENDS
Duneland
Outland Post
Mt. Kelsii
Cannondole
Elven Palace
The Great River
The Belirian Forest
Harpy's Point
The Neverending Sea
©2018 Jessica Khoury

The Deep of Tomorrow
The Wailing Cliffs
The Tutarian Mountains
The Lesser Tide
The Quiet Green
of Forever
CHARTILE

# CONTENTS

# PEOPLES

## PIPER ROMILLY

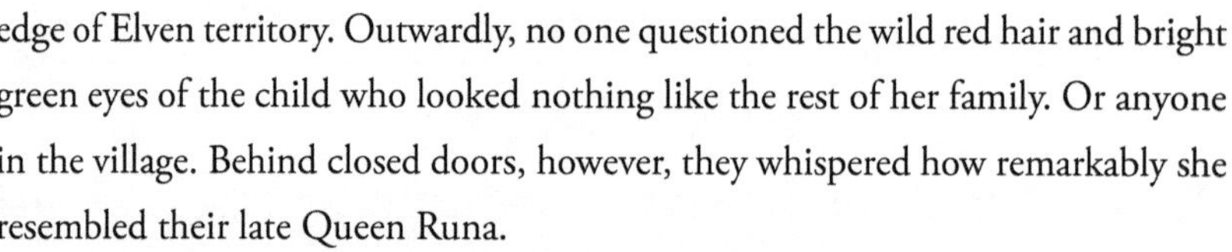

Born the second daughter of King
Aramor and Queen Runa
as Eva Ruani. At less than
two weeks old, the child was
named Piper by her adoptive
parents, Nevan and Paria Romilly. She
lived in Outland Post, a tiny village on the
edge of Elven territory. Outwardly, no one questioned the wild red hair and bright
green eyes of the child who looked nothing like the rest of her family. Or anyone
in the village. Behind closed doors, however, they whispered how remarkably she
resembled their late Queen Runa.

Unlike the other children in Outland Post, Piper was taught the many courtly
etiquettes of the Elven nobility. Her adoptive grandmother, Kaytah Chaudoin,
taught her to read and write the fancy calligraphy styles of the nobles. Piper often
accompanied Kaytah on trips across the Dwarvik and Elven territories of Chartile.

Though she took to her studies well, she more enjoyed working with her hands,
particularly making things in her father's smithy. She was a skilled archer and
often filled her pockets with pretty stones, even into adulthood.

Piper showed her first signs of magic at thirteen years old. Nevan, Paria,
and Kaytah attempted to keep her occupied with her etiquette studies, such as
learning the Dwarvik and Elven laws. But distractions did not keep her untrained
magic at bay.

Piper is often described as tenacious. She rarely asked for help, preferring to
work along. Her guarded demeanor made friendships difficult, even though she
cared deeply for her village. Even those who may have wronged her. It was for this
reason, the Incident at Outland Post occurred.

# JAYSON HILL

Jayson Michael Hill's most striking feature is not, in fact, his brilliant red hair, or the freckles scattered across his nose. Ask anyone who knows him, and they would immediately say it's his aptitude for being clumsy in any situation.

The Hills have lived in Swansdale for generations, most choosing to work in dental care.

Jayson has other ideas. He dreams of being a pilot in the air force, flying through the air at break-neck speeds in a fighter jet. His family will pat him on the back with a nod and a smile because it's difficult to tell where his jokes end and the truth begins. Anything can become a joke to Jayson Hill, as he uses comedy to mask his insecurities about never being good enough. Being the black-sheep in a long line of "perfect American families" is no easy expectation to live up to, which also makes Jayson quick to temper.

# LEONARDO DEHAVEN

As the son of two NASA scientists, Leonardo Isaac DeHaven approaches everything in life with a sort of linear logic. He moved to Swansdale from a small town near Las Vegas when he was ten years old with his father, Reagan DeHaven. Growing up close to the tourist attractions of Area 51, Leo has always held a secret fascination with historical conspiracies and the strange and unexplainable events in world history.

At twelve, Leo began teaching himself Sanskrit to read and decipher the ancient documents that supposedly mention extraterrestrial encounters he heard about at an art museum. Shortly after this, he received his first video game console, and rarely looked back at conspiracies until after his time spent in Chartile.

Leo is the spitting image of his father, from the messy blond hair, gray-blue eyes, and slightly pudgy physique. He bears little resemblance to his mother, Emily, but did inherit her natural ability to learn and decipher languages.

## JACK MITCHELL

Jack Anthony Mitchell dreams of a life in Hollywood. But's it's not the allure of paparazzi lights or red carpets. Though his wavy brown hair, dark eyes, and towering height would fit into any A-List celebrity lineup, Jack is a dreamer, a romantic, quiet and shy. He's an avid book reader and writer. He longs to escape to a world where he has control over what happens in a story—or a movie script, to be exact.

Jack's life has felt like chaos for as long as he can remember. At seven years old,

his family moved to Swansdale from Dover, Arkansas. This was the first time his father promised to "sober up," but it wouldn't be the last. Jack escaped into his books when his parents fought and argued. He'd climb beneath his bed, pulling the covers down to cover the gap, and read the books he hid there from his father's destructive hands. Later, Jack would learn to write his own poetry and stories as an outlet for the chaos and frustration his sensitive heart couldn't manage.

# DIMITRI

Simply referred to as "Dimitri" or "Head Retainer to The Empress," Dimitri was never given a surname, and no house or quarter ever claimed him. He was the illegitimate son of Empress Nefiri's youngest brother, Nahari, and her head retainer, Duj'anah.

Dimitri met Piper as a young child. She was seven years old, accompanying her grandmother for the first time on a trip to Mount Kelsii. The two became fast friends, and Nefiri permitted Dimitri to spend time with Piper in Outland Post, further cementing the two's relationship as they grew up.

When he was seventeen, Dimitri took up the role of Head Retainer to the Empress, like his mother, just before Piper was banished. Both loved and hated by the Dwarvik society, Dimitri was a constant, cruel reminder that even those voted to power could make mistakes. His charm and exceedingly handsome looks gave him an upper edge, especially with the Dwarvik women, for which he was not afraid to use to his advantage.

# ELVES

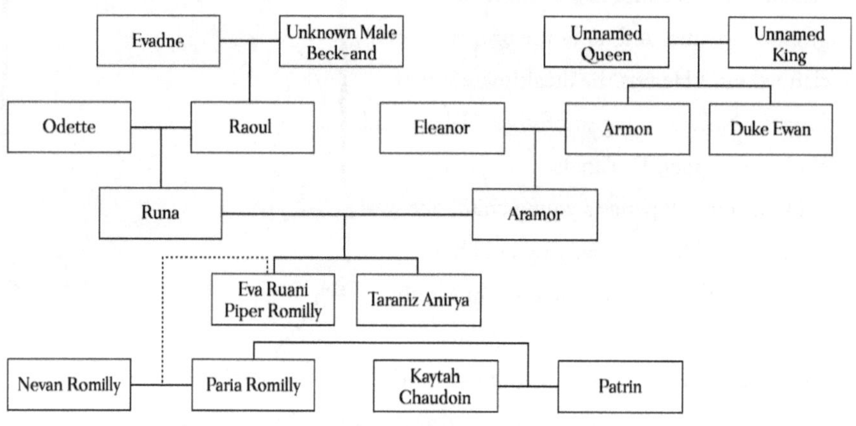

## PRINCESS TARANIZ ANIRYA

The first-born daughter of King Aramor and Queen Runa, Taraniz Anirya was, to any outsider looking in, a normal, young girl. She liked pretty things, especially shoes and bracelets, and even had a pet cat at one time. She was a quick learner. Managing the kingdom affairs came naturally. From nobles whose farms had not produced, to training regimens for the soldiers, Princess Taraniz had an instinct and knowledge beyond her years. She was also highly skilled with a *firon tutor* blade and dual-wielding daggers.

Taraniz, or Ani as her close family called her, began having strange dreams just before her twelfth birthday. She would awaken suddenly, screaming and thrashing in her bed, still seeing the images before her eyes. By the time she was thirteen, she had fallen into a great depression. Her once sweet and kind manner now cold and bitter. Her nightmares haunted her even when she was awake, manifesting as a voice that both taught and taunted her.

When Taraniz confided in her father of the darkness and the voice she fought each day, he shunned her. Afraid for both himself and his kingdom, he told

Taraniz to never speak of such things again. Taraniz felt betrayed and abandoned. Most of her friends had long since left her, as they too feared this strange power. Even Valar was of no comfort to her, having left several months prior with no explanation as to why.

Her fear grew to anger, and the soul of Duke Noraedin that resided within her grew stronger. At times, Taraniz felt powerful, longing for greater control over the amazing things the voice in her mind taught her to do with magic.

Soon, Taraniz realized the more she interacted with the voice, the more she seemed to lose moments of time. She could not recall what day it was, or how she had gotten to a particular location. She could no longer remember what she had been doing moments before, though it had been hours. When the hours turned to days, Taraniz fought against the voice with what little strength she had left.

Taraniz once regained control long enough to read the documents the voice in her mind tried to keep from her. Documents about a twin sister.

Months later, a messenger bird arrived at the palace requesting reinforcement for an incident at Outland Post. A girl they believed had the power of magic. A girl around the same age as the Elven princess. Determined to discover if this person might tell her who her sister was by using this supposed magic, Taraniz joined the party to Outland Post. But Duke Noraedin quickly took over her quest, and Taraniz did not regain herself again for several days until they were nearly back to the Elven Palace.

It is true that Taraniz wanted to bring the dwarves and elves under one rule. She hoped that by integrating some of the more "magical" and "mystical" practices of the dwarves into the elven culture, her people would one day become more open to allowing the practice of magic under intense restriction and supervision. It was how she had hoped to rid herself of the darkness in her mind.

# KING ARAMOR

The only child of King Armon and Queen Eleanor, Aramor had no cousins, and few uncles or aunts. He always knew he would be king but gave little thought to his future role until his father died unexpectedly of River Lung. Aramor did little to prepare himself for his reign and turned to his mother for guidance.

As the Conclave of Nobles was losing faith in Aramor, talks of finding Queen Eleanor a second husband were rampant. This course of action was rarely pursued, as it was believed to diminish the power of Elven bloodlines. Not just anyone could rule.

Queen Eleanor arranged the marriage between her son and the daughter of the Lord and Lady of Harpy's Pointee. The kindhearted spirit of Runa was well-known across the Elven territories, and Eleanor hoped the girl would settle her son and lead him to be more responsible. It was their love and respect for Runa that kept the Conclave from mutiny against Aramor.

# QUEEN RUNA

Lady Runa Elisa Vouclaine was the second child and first daughter of the Lord and Lady of Harpy's Pointee. She was gentle and kind and enjoyed playing along the banks of the Neverending Sea. As the daughter of a noble family, she was well-versed in the running of a household. She commanded respect with her family's beck-ands and servants but did not learn to read or write until she was much older.

It was long suspected that Runa would marry Valar, the son of the barony's tax collector, but when Queen Eleanor proposed the marriage between her son and Runa, the girl had little say in the matter.

Runa grew to care for her husband but could never love him. Their relationship was for convenience and for show, and behind closed doors, Runa sought emotional comfort in her childhood friend. She often blamed her inability to let go of Valar and learn to love Aramor on the magic she had inherited from her great-grandparents.

During her pregnancy, Runa suffered from what would later become known as Mother Melancholies. It was not the orenite cuffs the physicians refused to remove during childbirth that led to her death. It was this mental state, the unrequited love from Valar, and Aramor's complete disinterest in her.

# KING ARMON

Father to King Aramor, grandfather to Piper / Eva Ruani. King of the Elves of Chartile.

# QUEEN ELEANOR

Mother to King Aramor, grandmother to Piper / Eva Ruani. Queen of the Elves of Chartile.

# DUKE EWAN
## OF RUSHING REEDS PROVINCE

Uncle to King Aramor.

# LADY EVADNE
## RUNA'S GRANDMOTHER

Part of Piper/ Eva Ruani's namesake. Evadne's illegitimate relationship with a beck-and resulted in a child, though she was able to convince her husband it was his. Evanora's husband died only a few years later, and the truth came to light with close family only.

# LORD RAOUL

Father to Queen Runa, husband to Lady Odette, grandfather to Piper / Eva Ruani. The Lord of Harpy's Pointee.


# LADY ODETTE

Mother to Queen Runa, wife to Lord Raoul, grandmother to Piper / Eva Ruani. The Lady of Harpy's Pointee.

# KAYTAH CHAUDOIN

Kaytah Chaudoin was the daughter of a palace scribe and his wife, a successful herbalist from the Rushing Reeds Province. She met and married her husband, Patrin, at seventeen.

Deciding to follow in her father's footsteps, Kaytah became a scribe within the community. Patrin supported her ambitions to become a palace scribe. He took on many of the responsibilities of caring for their daughter, Paria, and was happy to do so. He passed in a fishing accident when Paria was three years old, leaving Paria's care in the hands of her grandparents.

Kaytah retired from scribal work after the Incident at Outland Post. There, she took over as the healing woman in the village and cared for Piper from a distance.


# NEVAN ROMILLY

Descended from a family of smiths who had lived in Outland Post for generations, Nevan Romilly met his wife, Paria, when Kaytah came to do a census of the village and brought her daughter along.

Nevan was a simple man, dedicated to his work and family. He had an affinity for working with soft metals to make feastware and betrothal gifts.

Outland Post's location between Mount Kelsii and Duneland made purchasing second-hand and discarded remnants of gem fragments and metals inexpensive. This allowed the Romilly family to sell their goods at a lower cost to the local and surrounding towns as opposed to importing from Duneland or directly from the Dwarves. However, because the materials were second-hand, the quality wasn't always as well-made, making the pieces more attractive to lower and middle-class buyers. Noble and Royal families would not have purchased such goods.

Nevan held an attention to detail that surpassed his father's, making his betrothal gifts, and the designs on his feastware easily identifiable in the region. It was likely a contributing factor to Piper's taste for intricate designs in her jewelry and embroidery.

He was initially against adopting Piper and was emotionally distant to her for the first few years of her life. But the two grew close with time, and he even taught her green and white smithing techniques. As she grew older, he enjoyed shooting archery with her in their free time, and Piper could be frequently found working the bellows as Nevan's shadow.

# PARIA ROMILLY

Paria Chaudoin (later Romilly) was the daughter of a palace scribe and local fisherman, and the granddaughter of a palace scribe and herbalist from The Rushing Reeds Province. Paria was mostly raised by her grandparents after her father drowned in a fishing accident when she was three years old. Her mother continued to work as a palace scribe and traveled all over the Elven territories of Chartile, sometimes bringing her daughter once she was older. Paria met Nevan while accompanying her mother on a trip to Outland Post. Paria followed in her grandmother's footsteps as an herbalist and was one of the main healers in Outland Post.

## PATRIN

Husband to Kaytah, Father of Paria. A fisherman from the Rushing Reeds Province area. He passed in a fishing accident when Paria was three years old, leaving Paria's care in the hands of her grandparents.

## VALAR MARION

Valar Marion grew up as the son of a tax collector in Harpy's Pointee. He spent his early years as a typical child of a lower class noble and would often play along the shores with his friend, Runa. His adolescent years quickly turned to rigorous studies which would prepare him to succeed his childless and aging uncle as the Lord of Cannondole. It was a role no one anticipated him having to take on.

Years later, Runa was betrothed to then Prince Aramor. It was she who got her old friend appointed as the King's Head Advisor shortly after marriage when Aramor's advisor at the time retired. It was this decision that brought the childhood friends close again, and which created tensions between Valar and his wife, Aylin.

Valar became a second father to Princess Taraniz after Runa's death. And when the soul of Duke Noraedin overtook Taraniz, Valar was the only person who could help her overcome the control Noraedin had over her. As Noraedin's soul grew strong, Valar realized there was little more he could do to save her. At first, he hoped Piper could help Taraniz, as he knew of her magical abilities from Kaytah. But when it soon became clear Taraniz was beyond anyone's help. Heartbroken, he began putting plans into motion that would help Piper ascend the throne and usurp Taraniz.

After Noraedin's defeat, Valar returned to his role as Lord of Cannondole. He had had enough of kingdom politics and was content to work within the confines of his own town. He spent his time with Brock's father and enjoyed vinting various sweet wines.

# VALIN MARION

Though Valin always knew he'd one day become Lord of Cannondole, it didn't stop him from enjoying his youth. He was the only child of Valar and Aylin Marion. His parents met when they were twenty years old, married shortly thereafter, and gave birth to Valin exactly one year later. Many believed Valin's wild spirit and rebellious behavior were the product of his parents' quick marriage, which came as a result of Valar's jealousy over losing Runa to Aramor.

Valin became the Lord of Cannondole when he was only twelve years old, after Valin became the Head Advisor to the King. But holding a title and carrying out the duties of an office are two different matters entirely. It was Aylin who governed Cannondole through her son. Valin had little interest in the politics and operations of the town he inherited. Instead, he found comfort in a string of lovers as a teenager and frequently gambled away the family's personal coffers disguised in the taverns of neighboring towns. It wasn't until Aylin was stricken with the Five-Day Fever and died was Valin forced to assume the responsibilities he had been shirking. He was nineteen. His experience beguiling both men and maidens gave him an edge in negotiations both in his short time as Lord and later as King.

# AYLIN

Mother of Valin Marion, wife to Valar Marion. Aylin was primarily responsible for managing the affairs of Cannondole when her husband was appointed as the head advisor to King Aramor. She died of the Five-Day Fever when her son was nineteen, forcing him to finally take up the role he had ignored with abandon for so long.

# ATANA JAMESON

Atana "Addie" Jameson is the eldest of three daughters to Aiden and Lana Jameson. Her family have been fishermen along the Great River for generations.

# ARDA JAMESON

Arda "Ardy" Jameson is the second-born daughter to Aiden and Lana Jameson, and Atana "Addie's" sister. She would later become the healer for Cannondole.

# ALMARA JAMESON

Almara "Ally" Jameson is the third-born daughter to Aiden and Lana Jameson, and Atana "Addie's" youngest sister. She would later become the mistress to Geofrey Garrigs, the Captain of the Elven Guard, passing valuable information to her sisters about the happenings at the Elven court.

# AIDEN JAMESON

Father to Atana "Addie," Arda "Ardy," and Almara "Ally" Jameson. Husband to Lana Jameson. Works as a fisherman on the Great River a few days' journey outside Cannondole.

# LANA JAMESON

Mother to Atana "Addie," Arda "Ardy," and Almara "Ally" Jameson. Wife to Aiden Jameson.

# BRODRICK GARRISON

The son of a local vinter in Cannondole. Brodrick did not sit idly by and live off his parents' coin. Brock was extremely ambitious, even at a young age. He did odd jobs for the merchants and business owners in Cannondole, including delivering medicines from the local apothecary and caring for the horses and stable at The Glass Lantern.

# TATHIAS

An Elven soldier, manipulated by Noraedin through Taraniz to work in secret with the dwarves. His mission to infiltrate Mount Kelsii was made with the promise he would rejoin his family – whom had been killed by Taraniz under Noraedin's manipulation – in the afterlife.

# SISTER THEODORA

One of the Sisters of the Chantry of Canna. She particularly likes to garden.

# SISTER MARTA

One of the Sisters of the Chantry of Canna. She likes to read and write.

# MATTIMORE ROUX

A first-rate rogue. Mattimore earns his coin at various jobs, and just as quickly spends it away. He has traveled all over Chartile and has been caught by the local soldiers of several towns for stealing or fighting. His most recent antics of attempting to walk onto the palace grounds rather drunk, with the intention of marrying Princess Taraniz, landed him in the palace dungeons.

# LELAND
## CAPTAIN OF THE ELVEN GUARD

Leland took command of the guards of the palace and the movements of the elven armies when Taraniz – under the influence of Noraedin – killed the previous Captain. Leland was rather young for the position but did well for himself, especially after Piper took the throne.

# GEOFREY GARRIGS

Became Captain of the Elven Guard when Captain Leland resigned his commission. Though a married man, Geofrey became acquainted with Ally

Jameson, a lady in waiting for a lesser noble.

## CHAMBERLAIN HERODAN

Appointed as the caretaker of Duneland by Nefiri, Aramor, and Runa. Herodan was first a Baron Flame's Bough and a member of the Council of Elders.

# DWARVES

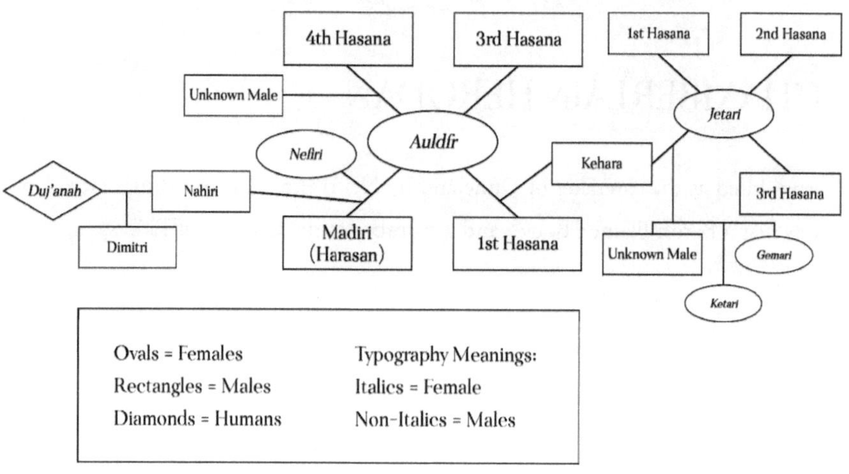


## EMPRESS NEFIRI
## OF THE HOUSE OF AULDFR

Nefiri is the fourth-born child and the first-born daughter of Auldfr, and the second-born child of Auldfr's second hasana (Harasan at the time of her birth), Madiri.

The Council of Elders chose Nefiri to train as a Princess of Mount Kelsii when she was five years old. Shortly thereafter, most of Nefiri's brothers trained in the Royal Guard and became her personal guard. When she was twenty, Nefiri chose to be trained in Peace and became Princess when she was Twenty-nine, succeeding Queen Carendeil.

As a royal, Nefiri could not lawfully engage in a romantic relationship or bear children. It was her disdain for this Dwarvik law that allowed her to turn a blind eye to the illegitimate relationship between her brother, Nahiri, and her Human Head Retainer, Duj'anah. She refused to deny Nahiri his love for Duj'anah, since her own ability to love had been taken from her when she was too little to know better.

When the two were discovered, and the subsequent birth of Dimitri occured, Nefiri felt guilty for not doing her part to end things when she had the chance.

To her, Dimitri was not the mistake of Nahiri and Duj'anah, but the mistake of a royal. This is why she raised Dimitri.

Nefiri often found peace while consulting the Oracle to speak with Rashiri. She specifically requested to be trained in its use. After her retirement as Empress, Nefiri became a priestess of Rashiri, and honed her skills in using the Oracle.

# AULDFR

Mother to Empress Nefiri, and wife to Madiri, her second hasana and later Harasan at Nefiri's birth.

# MADIRI

Father to Empress Nefiri and second hasana, later Harasan, to Auldfr.

# KEHARA

Fourth hasana to Jetari, and father to Ketari and Princess Gemari. Brother to Empress Nefiri.

# JETARI

Mother to Princess Gemari and Ketari, and wife to fourth hasana, Kehara.

# NAHIRI

The eighth born child, and seventh born son of Auldfr and the third-born child of Madiri. Nahiri was a dedicated guard to his older sister, Empress Nefiri. Though

Auldfr attempted many matches for her son, Nahiri turned them all down, instead, dedicating himself to his work of protecting his sister.

It was during a trip to Duneland to acquire more beck-ands that Nahiri first set eyes on Duj'anah. He was immediately struck by her beauty in a way he had never felt before. At night, he would sneak away to her holding cell and sit outside the bars of the prison, speaking late into the darkness. On Bidding Day, Nahiri begged his sister to purchase Duj'anah, to which she obliged.

Once they returned, Nahiri continued his nightly visits with Duj'anah in secret. He educated her on the small idiosyncrasies of his sister, helping Duj'anah move up in the ranks of the beck-ands and eventually acquire her position as Nefiri's head retainer, a position typically held by other dwarves.

Nefiri discovered Nahiri and Duj'anah's relationship when she unexpectedly returned to her quarters to retrieve a document she needed for a meeting but had forgotten. Nahiri again begged to his sister, but this time, it was for Duj'anah's life. Relationships with Humans was illegal, and the punishment for both of them was death. Nefiri assured her little brother she would not turn them in but cautioned them to be more discreet.

Years passed before Nefiri and Duj'anah were discovered again. Though Nefiri tried to advocate for Nahiri and Duj'anah, it was to no avail. The last words he ever spoke to Duj'anah were, "in this life or the next, I will find you." He was unaware she was with child.

# PRINCESS GEMARI
## OF THE HOUSE OF JETARI

Gemari is the third-born child and the second-born daughter of Jetari, and the first-born child of Jetari's fourth hasana, Kehara.

She was chosen by the Council at age five to train as a Princess of Mount Kelsii, and at age sixteen, Gemari chose to be trained in the ways of Peace, like her aunt, the Empress Nefiri. By age seventeen, Gemari had succeeded Princess Thora as the Princess to Mount Kelsii after Thora's death resulting from a tunnel collapse.

Three years later, Gemari worked with the Council of Elders to reconstruct some of the old, abandoned mines for the safety of the Mount Kelsii citizens and the integrity of the mountain itself. Unbeknownst to her, these mines were later occupied in secret by the Black Diamonds.

Having been thrust into her position of power and responsibility at such a young age, Gemari never experienced much in the way of a childhood. She always felt rather naïve and out of place, being the youngest among her peers. Meeting Jack and learning more about the Black Diamonds allowed her to see the world in a different light. She felt the weight of her position in a way she never had before and went on to become one of the most beloved and well-known Queens of Mount Kelsii.

# KETARI

The first-born daughter to Jetari and her fourth hasana, Kehara, who is also Nefiri's second-eldest brother. The Council considered Ketari too rigid for selection in training for princesshood. Instead, Ketari trained as a retainer for the Royalty.

When Gemari was elected as Princess of Mount Kelsii, it was decided Ketari would be her Head Retainer.

Ketari often helped and guided her little sister in making important decisions early in her career. Though the two often disagreed, they shared an unspoken affection and loyalty to one another.

# QUEEN UNA
## OF THE HOUSE OF ULFRA

Though Una was not the first-born daughter of the House of Ulfra, she felt the same pressures, if not more so, to make a name for her House among the quarters.

Una was the second-born daughter to Ulfra and her second hasana, Bragrin. Ulfra suffered a miscarriage with her first daughter, thus thrusting perfection upon Una.

At fourteen, Una insisted on training in both Peace and War. Her mother did not believe she was up for such a challenge, and that doing so would affect her prospects of being chosen as Princess. Una resolved to prove her mother wrong and succeeded.

Una's mother showed little affection for her daughter, recognizing instead that her birth was an opportunity. An opportunity to not only advance the status of her house but also an opportunity to increase their wealth. With each advancement Una achieved, the more Ulfra could negotiate for higher positions, higher pay, and even a larger homestead.

This left Una with a rather bitter disposition toward everyone she met, as it was the demeanor she always received from her mother. However, her direct approach to problems and dissociation from her emotions allowed her to present and carry out solutions that were not impeded by a personal agenda.

When Ulfra returned to the stone, it left Una with the additional responsibility to care for father and her mother's other hasanas as they had no other children.

## ULFRA

Mother to Queen Una, and wife to Bragrin, her first hasana.

## BRAGRIN

Father to Queen Una, and first hasana to Ulfra.

## QUEEN ISLA
### OF THE HOUSE OF ARNKATLA

Isla experienced a very different upbringing from most Dwarvik children. Instead of adhering to the strict beliefs of the matriarchal-run society, she was brought up to believe in equality and love above all else.

She was born the first child of Arnkatla and her first and only hasana (Harasan at Isla's birth), Esjani. Secretly, they were the first to work towards creating a coalition that advocated the beliefs of the Black Diamonds.

Isla's parents trained and guided her tirelessly from birth in the hopes the Council would select her for additional training. When she was, Arnkatla and Esjani continued their influence on her training through her teachers and trusted Elders.

Though few ever knew, not even her own parents, Isla taught herself the traditional ceremonial dances of her people. She loved to dance and believed she may have become an entertainer if her life had turned out differently. She met Kylani, her future lover, one night when she snuck away to an abandoned mine to dance in secret.

# ARNKATLA

Mother to Queen Isla, and wife to her only hasana, later Harasan, Esjani. Arnkatla and her husband were integral founders of the Black Diamonds and the movement toward equality that they represented. She often visited the Oracle and left offerings to the Goddesses that the Council would choose her daughter to train as a royal.

Knowing that even if she was not chosen to succeed Queen Carendeil, her daughter would then likely hold an Elder position. Though her objective to strategically use her daughter to further her and Esjani's cause was always at the forefront of her mind, she never lost sight of doting unconditional love and support to Isla.

When Gudvor and Faerdir were killed, they helped Faeridae find new matches for the girl's father, brothers, and Gudvor's other hasanas, most of which were also strategically placed to further their efforts.

# ESJANI

Father to Queen Isla and only hasana, later Harasan, to Arnkatla. Edjani and Arnkatla were integral founders of the Black Diamonds. Many argue the ideas of equality between Dwarvik men and women was nothing new, but something only spoken in the shadows. It was Esjani who gave a voice and a platform to those ideas, further shaping them and providing a structure on which to grow. He supported his wife's idea to position Isla within a place of power.

# PRINCESS FAERIDAE
## OF THE HOUSE OF GUDVOR

Faeridae was the first-born daughter of Gudvor and her second hasana (Harasan at Faeridae's birth), Faerdir. Though she was fourteen years old, Isla was Faeridae's dearest friend. Faeridae was one of few who knew of Isla's love of dancing.

The Council selected Faeridae to train as a Princess of the Tutarian Mountains when she was five. With growing tensions between the Black Diamonds and the Council of Elders, Faeridae felt being trained in War, like Queen Carendeil, was the wisest decision. Her parents, however, were not happy with this decision. They felt they had failed their daughter by not instilling a want of peace and harmony within her.

Faeridae's parents and one of her brothers were killed during a raid by the Kelsii soldiers when their secret location within the mountain was discovered. Faeridae turned to Arnkatla and Esjani for assistance in arranging new marriages for Gudvor's remaining hasanas and a few of her brothers who were not yet married.

# GUDVOR

Mother of Princess Faeridae and wife to Faerdir, her second hasana, later Harasan. Friend to Arnkatla and Esjani. Gudvor was killed in a raid by Kelsii soldiers when the current hideout of the Black Diamonds was discovered.

# FAERDIR

Father to Princess Faeridae and second hasana, later Harasan, to Gudvor. Faeridae was friends with Esjani growing up and introduced his wife to Arnkatla and Esjani in the hopes the two could sway her toward their beliefs of equality. Gudvor did come to hold the beliefs and values of the Black Diamonds, but she did not wish Faeridae to be raised as Isla had been, much to Faeridir's regret. Faerdir was killed in a raid by Kelsii soldiers along with his wife when the current meeting place of the Black Diamonds was discovered in an abandoned mine.

# BRANDE
## OF THE HOUSE OF KYMORA

Brande was born the fourth son of Kymora and her third hasana, Bairdir.

His entire life, Brande wanted nothing more than to be a Kelsii soldier, like his two older brothers. He worked hard, and trained every day, but was still denied the position when he was fifteen. He did not meet the height requirement by a finger's width.

Completely distraught, and with seeming no direction in his life, Brande left home. He lived on the outskirts of the Belirian Forest close to the mountain for over three weeks. His brother, Kylani, found him and confided in Brande his involvement with the Black Diamonds. Brande felt a renewed purpose in his life.

He worked alongside Kylani as a miner and falsified his death in the accident that killed Faeridae's parents. After which, he worked quietly alongside his brother to bring more members into the Black Diamonds.

Eventually, Brande did gain the extra height that would have been needed to join the Kelsii soldiers.

# KYLANI
## OF THE HOUSE OF KYMORA

Kylani is the third-born son of Kymora and her fourth hasana, Oslani. Kylani's two eldest brothers were accepted to train as Kelsii soldiers at a very young age. This left Kylani to help his father and his mother's other hasanas to care for his younger brothers and baby sister.

Kylani showed an interest in medicine very early and trained under one of Kelsii's healers by the age of twelve. This left him little time to spend at home, and he felt entirely responsible when his little brother and best friend, Brande, ran away from home a few years later.

While looking for his brother, Kylani discovered Isla dancing in an abandoned mine. They met secretly every day for over a week, during which she taught him about her beliefs and the Black Diamonds. With Isla's help, Kylani found Brande living at the base of the mountain in the Belirian Forest. He convinced Brande to come back home with the hopes of them joining the Black Diamonds. Kylani and Isla's secret meetings continued for years.

He faked his death during the mine collapse that killed Faeridae's parents. He then worked and lived with the Black Diamonds in secret full-time along with his brother and was able to pursue a deeper relationship with Isla.

# KYMORA

Mother of Kylani and Brande, and wife to Bairdir, her third hasana, and Oslani, her fourth hasana.

# BAIRDIR

Father of Brande, and third hasana to Kymora.

# OSLANI

Father of Kylani, and fourth hasana to Kymora

# IMOHAN
## OF THE HOUSE OF ALOFRAH
## ELDER OF THE OPAL QUARTER

Daughter of Alofrah and her third hasana, Imojarah. Elder of the Opal Quarter of the Tutarian Mountains.

# IMOHAD

Third Hasana of House Alofrah. Younger brother to Elder Imohan of the Topaz Quarter of Mount Kelsii. Imohad worked as a soldier his entire life.


# ALOFRAH

Mother of Elder Imohan of the Opal Quarter and Imohad, and wife of Imojarah.


# IMOJARAH

Father of Elder Imohan of the Opal Quarter and Imohad, and third hasana of Alofrah.

# FREJAH
## OF THE HOUSE OF BERKHILDR
## OF THE CARNELIAN QUARTER

First daughter of Berkhildr, a previous elder of the Carnelian Quarter. Frejah always knew she wanted to be an elder. It took her some time to decide if she wanted to marry. Frejah eventually took two hasanas. Both outlived her. She had three sons and no daughters.


# BERKHILDR

Mother of Elder Frejah of the Carnelian Quarter.

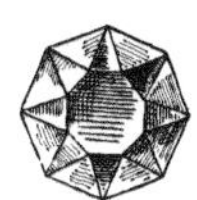

# ULFWYN
## OF THE HOUSE OF HALLVOR
## OF THE COBALT QUARTER

Second daughter of Hallvor and her Harasan, Ulfrik. Ulfwyn took no husbands. Rumors say she bore one illegitimate child, but it was never proven.

# HALLVOR

Mother of Elder Ulfwyn of the Cobalt Quarter, and wife of Ulfrik.

# ULFRIK

Father of Elder Ulfwyn of the Cobalt Quarter, and harasan to Hallvor.

# JARVAE
## OF THE HOUSE OF JARLIL
## ELDER OF THE GARNET QUARTER

Daughter of Jarlil and her second hasana, Torvae. Jarvae was the elder of Garnet Quarter of the Tutarian Mountains. She took her first hasana very early in life and eventually took three more. She was blessed with two daughters and seven sons.

# JARLIL

Mother of Elder Jarvae of the Garnet Quarter, and wife of Torvae.


# TORVAE

Father of Elder Jarvae of the Garnet Quarter, and second hasana to Jarlil.

# YGDALLA
## OF THE HOUSE OF DRYFINAL
## OF THE AMETHYST QUARTER

Ygdalla was the first-born daughter of Dryfinal and her Harasan, Yngvarr. Ygdalla was an only child for many years, as her mother did not wish to take any more husbands.

Ygdalla was assaulted and violated by a soldier when she was seventeen years old. From that point onward, Ygdalla embraced her femininity and used the position of power she knew she held as a woman against anyone who tried to defy her.

It was Isla who tempered Ygdalla's rage and anger, teaching her how to make more calculated decisions. Ygdalla eventually supported Isla's underground movement of getting a male voice on the Council, but a part of her that only agreed so she could prove how superior a woman was to a man.

Ygdalla married in time, but only took one hasana, like her mother. She trusted her husband and wasn't sure she could ever trust anyone else so wholly without the risk of being hurt again.

# DRYFINAL

Mother of Elder Ygdalla of the Amethyst Quarter, and wife of Yngvarr, her only husband.

# YNGVARR

Father of Elder Ygdalla of the Amethyst Quarter, and harasan to Dryfinal.

# AERNDIS

The first daughter of a wealthy family in the Ruby Quarter, Aerndis had taken two husbands by the time she was thirty-one, and the other two followed suit shortly thereafter. She bore two daughters and thirteen sons. She held significant influence within the Ruby Quarter, often bribing and manipulating whoever held the Elder seat of her quarter at the time.

# AERIS

The second daughter of a wealthy family in the Ruby Quarter, Aeris was the opposite of her older sister, Aerndis. She married late in life, having only two husbands, four sons, and no daughters.

Aeris's first husband was recruited to the Black Diamonds as an inside source within the Palace Guards. He confided this to Aeris shortly after their marriage, and they quietly supported the efforts of the Black Diamonds together. Aeris worked hard to undermine all her sister attempted to do to further the cause of executing all the Black Diamonds.

# AVANTRIA

Daughter of Aerndis. She courted Orctkar as a teenager, but her match to him was refused in leu of Neradah, who was older and with an established House. She continued to see him for years, even after each had married and bore children within their respective houses, feeling a sense of entitlement and possession of Orctkar.

# ORCTKAR

Son of Balla and her first hasana, Otkatir, Orctkar showed great interest in working with food from a young age. He worked along the mountainside with the farmers as an early teenager. Balla found him an apprenticeship working in the kitchens at Mount Kelsii. Orctkar went on to marry Neradah and became Harasan to her House.

# BALLA

Mother of Orctkar, and wife of Otkatir.

# OTKATIR

Father of Orctkar, and first hasana to Balla

# NERADAH

Wife of Orctkar.

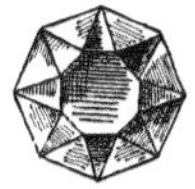

# QUEEN CARENDEIL
## OF THE HOUSE OF ESJAMOURN

Queen of the Tutarian Mountains, Carendeil passed back to the stone from The Five-Day Fever. She was rather young, and her death came as a great shock to the Dwarvik community. She was succeeded by Queen Isla.

# ESJAMOURN

Mother of Queen Carendeil.

# LYNDEN
## OF THE HOUSE OF LYNHLDR

The sole survivor of a tragic altercation between the soldiers of Mount Kelsii and The Black Diamonds in the Ruby Quarter. Lynden hid inside a cabinet during the altercation and watched her entire family slaughtered through the crack between the doors.

# LYNHLDR

Mother of Lynden. The victim of an altercation between the Black Diamonds and the Mount Kelsii Soldiers in the Ruby Quarter. The incident surrounded her third hasana, who discovered his wife and her other husbands had been working with The Black Diamonds. He coordinated an attack on the household. He felt remorse and informed the family at the last moment before the attack. He hoped they could all flee into the Belirian Forest and start a new life elsewhere. The soldiers attacked before they could leave.

# MALTORI

Second Hasana to the House of Arnfastah. Maltori worked as a blacksmith for Mount Kelsii, often repairing the soldiers' armor. He turned spy for the Black Diamonds after Princess Thora's death. He later became an informant for Princess Taraniz when he heard her plans to unite the Dwarves and Elves under a single rule. Maltori always placed his bets with the biggest fish and the highest bidder.

# ARNFASTAH

Wife of Maltori, her second hasana.

# HALIL
## COMMANDER OF THE GUARD

Harasan of The House of Isanorah of the Amber Quarter. Halil was father to one daughter and two sons. He held his position as Commander of the Guard into his sixties. He finally retired once he developed Thyruni's Jewels.

# ISANORAH

Wife of Halil, Commander of the Royal Guard of Mount Kelsii.

# PRINCESS THORA

Princess Thora of Mount Kelsii, passed in a tragic cave-in that killed her and her entire guard. Rumor and speculation say it was for her involvement with the Black Diamonds. Some believe several Council Elders planned the accident and subsequently blamed the Black Diamonds. However, there is no proof of this. She was succeeded by Princess Gemari.

# TAGRIN

A soldier of Mount Kelsii. His brother was killed in a sabotage by the Black Diamonds, and he forever held the deepest hatred toward the organization.

# SINTORI

Harasan of House Geofra, Sintora was the historian for Mount Kelsii.

# JENTAR

A longtime supporter of The Black Diamonds. Jentar learned his trade as a blacksmith and armorer, then faked his death in a skirmish between the Mount Kelsii soldiers and a group of Black Diamonds. Since that time, he has sold weapons to the rogue organization using the connections he still had to those working in secret in Mount Kelsii. He expanded his reach into the Tutarian Mountains to obtain other supplies with some of the traveling merchants. He even worked through Queen Isla and Princess Faeridae. Jentar never married but eventually began a relationship with a human slave much later in life.

# EARTH FAMILY AND KIN

## REAGAN DEHAVEN

In the early 1970's Reagan DeHaven moved to the United Kingdom to live with his grandparents, and attend Cambridge University, a long-standing DeHaven family tradition. He received his PhD in Engineering with a minor in Quantum Physics before moving back to the US. He lived with his parents in their retirement home in Las Vegas. Reagan had difficulty finding work in his field, and resigned himself to teaching mathematics at a local community college until he received a job offer from NASA in the mid 1980's. He met his wife while working on their project, P905-Tes.

Reagan is highly intelligent, if sometimes naïve. He sees the good in people and works hard to bring it out in them.

## EMILY DEHAVEN

The adopted daughter of a successful casino owner, Emily Ward (later DeHaven) was expected to take over the family business. When she decided to change her business major to a degree in Physics, the family disowned her, and she never spoke to them again. She met her husband thirteen years later while working for NASA on the P905-Tes project. Her family never knew she married or had a child.

When P905-Tes was canceled, and Emily and Reagan were dismissed from work, Emily immediately contacted friends she had in France and found a job at CERN. Heartbroken, Emily left her husband and son behind, hoping to return to them one day.

# DAVID HILL

David Hill was a software programmer that worked from home, giving him the ability to take his daughter, Jessica, to her specialty school in Michigan. He later went on to work for the Apple Corporation after his children had graduated high school.

# SUSAN HILL

Susan Cancio (later Hill) was a dental hygienist like her mother before her, working at the same dentist's office her mother had years ago. Her family had lived in Swansdale for several generations. She and David did not leave until after Jayson had bought their home from them when David was offered a job by Apple. It was one of the only times Susan had ever left Ohio, save for the couple trips across the border to Michigan for her daughter's school activities.

# CARTER MITCHELL

If you were to ask anyone in the Mitchell family, they'd tell you none of them were important – especially Carter. Too skinny, too sun-tanned, and too sensitive, they'd say. After suffering years of physical abuse from his alcoholic father – who had tried for years to "beat the sissy out of him" – Carter began drinking at the age of fifteen. Despite every effort to not be like his father, it was the only thing that seemed to make Carter's father believe he was finally a man, and the two finally bonded over nights sitting on the back porch drinking.

Carter found a job at a local gas station in Dover, Arkansas as a mechanic. He met his wife, Karla, when her car was towed into the shop. It was love at first sight, and Karla never returned to her home in Maine.

Carter lost his job after only six months. It was Karla who broke through the shell he'd built around himself. She convinced him to get clean and sober up. He was successful for nearly a year. Unable to find work, however, they decided to move to Ohio, where there were more automotive jobs available in the early 1980's.

# KARLA MITCHELL

Karla Franklin (later Mitchell) was the youngest of five sisters and the only one to graduate college. Her family never supported her endeavors to waste her money on a college education when she would have been perfectly secure in money and life working at her family's historical Bed and Breakfast in Camden, Maine. But the tenacious young girl had other ideas. Graduating at the top of her class with *magna cum laude* honors, Karla took off with her friends for a much-needed escape. When their car broke down, Karla met her future husband, the young mechanic at the small gas station up the road. Two years later, they were married with their first child, Jack, on the way.

Karla knew about Carter's drinking habits from the very beginning of their relationship. However, she refused to admit her family had been right about marrying "that redneck boy," and would not abandon him.


# JESSICA HILL

Younger sister to Jayson Hill, and youngest daughter to David and Susan Hill. She graduated early from Cranbrook and attended Brown University in Rhode Island for which she received an MFA. Her acting career mostly consisted of commercials and a year traveling in a production of *Six*. In her mid-twenties, Jessica went back to school, earning her PhD in psychiatry with a minor in astronomy from Georgetown University. She lived a busy life in Washington, DC, forever holding a flame for Jack Mitchell. She occupied herself with her work, which she spoke rarely of at family events.

# STEPHANIE MITCHELL

Younger sister to Jack Mitchell, older sister to a little brother, and the only daughter of Carter and Karla Mitchel. The chaos of Stephanie's home life was unkind to her. She experimented in middle school and high school with a plethora of illegal substances and activities.

Unable to live up to her older brother's success, and feeling forgotten when her baby brother was born, Stephanie dropped out of school as soon as she was eighteen, and left Ohio for Arkansas, hoping distance and time would heal her troubles. She spent much of her adult life in and out of rehab, often paid for by her older brother, until she took her life from an intentional drug overdose when she was in her late thirties.

# UNCLE ROB

Uncle to Jack Mitchell, husband of Kiera Franklin (later Paulicki). Rob worked as an insurance agent in Camden, Maine.

# AUNT KIERA

Aunt to Jack Mitchell, wife of Robert Paulicki. Kiera worked part-time as a travel agent, and as a guest concierge at her family's bed and breakfast.

# MR. DARROW

History unknown.

# MS. PINCE

One of the librarians at the Swansdale Public Library. She dedicated her life to the library and was constantly passed over for promotions for one reason or another.

40

# PLACES

## THE ELVEN PALACE

It is unknown when the Elven palace was first built, though 'built' is a loose term. It is believed magic was once used to weave the branches of the surrounding trees together and strengthen the trunks of the belirian trees. As the races evolved their culture and societies, it became necessary for the tree-dwelling race of Elves to create a central location that other races could access more easily. Legend says the Elven throne was the first tree to grow from the tears of the Phoenix and bear the first of the Elven race.

## THE BELIRIAN FOREST

The first and heart of the Elven territories. The trees of the forest are so large, the elves built their homes both in the boughs, and the trunks.

## OUTLAND POST

A small village at the base of Mount Kelsii. Once a Human community, it was claimed by the Elves after the defeat of Noraedin as a strategic move to secure an Elven presence between Duneland (previously Nazarakapi) and the Dwarves' recent territory claim of Mount Kelsii. It is unusual for an Elven community to be so far removed from the forest.

# THE GLASS LANTERN

The Glass Lantern is one of the oldest pubs and inns in the Elven territories. Identified by the glass lantern that always burns outside the front door.

# CANNONDOLE

Elven town located between the Great River and the Belirian Forest. Home to Valar, advisor to King Aramor, and his son Valin.

# HARPY'S POINTE

Once a coastal city belonging to the Merfolk, Harpy's Pointe sits on the edge of the Neverending Sea and the estuary between the sea and the Great River. The castle of Harpy's Pointe sits at the edge of a cliff. Once believed to have been built by the Harpy heckle (or flock) that resided along the rocky coast, a single, narrow road was later added. Only wide enough for an individual to access by walking single file, and too small for horses, wagons, or carts to traverse. It's adjoining town was, and still is, a central hub or trade along the coasts and up the river.

# THE RUSHING REEDS PROVINCE

Birthplace of Kaytah Chaudoin. Located at the edge of the Belirian Forest and the Ivory Cove. During the Melt Moon and Flood Moon, the area frequently floods, creating a kind of Bayou that nourishes the soil of much needed minerals for the upcoming growing season. Its climate is similar to Harpy's Pointe, and is an area known for its herbal medicine and sweet wines.

# BARONY OF FLAME'S BOUGH

Located in the heart of the Belirian Forest, and home to some of the oldest Elven settlements in Chartile. The home of Chamberlain Herodan.

# THE IVORY COVE

Located in the Rushing Reeds Province and fed by the Neverending Sea.

# CASTIELLE

Elven town located on the Palace side of the Great River.

# SERESTELL

Elven town located on the Palace side of the Great River.

# DUNELAND

The name given to the Human territories of Chartile after the defeat of Noraedin.

After the Great War, when Humans were forced into slavery, much of Humanity's culture was erased, including the names of their cities, towns, and the name of their Kingdom. It is now a neutral territory between the Elves and Dwarves, with alternating leadership appointed by the Dwarvik and Elven royalty.

## NAZARAKAPI

The name given to the Human territories of Chartile during the time of the four kings. After the Great War, when Humans were forced into slavery, much of Humanity's culture was erased, including the names of their cities, towns, and the name of their Kingdom. Renamed Duneland.

## THE BAY OF TAL ISK'JABAR

Located on the Nazarakapi edge of the Wailing Cliffs, the Bay of Tal Isk'jabar is a recessed coastal body of water connected to the Neverending Sea. It is home to a variety of unique marine-life and a thriving coastal city.

# THE WAILING CLIFFS

A massive expanse of miles-high cliffs that run the length of Chartile from the Bay of Tal Isk'jabar to The Deep of Tomorrow in the ancient Merfolk Kingdom. Named for sound made by the constant wind that sounded as if a thousand souls were screaming or wailing. After the Great War had ended, the many magical creatures of Chartile disappeared behind the towering walls of the Wailing Cliffs. Anyone who dared to scale them was never heard from again.

# MOUNT KELSII

A single mountain at the edge of the old Human territories. Between the Wailing Cliffs, The Great Plains, and Duneland (previously Nazarakapi). At a fraction of the size of Tutaria, Mount Kelsii was claimed mostly for trading purposes as opposed to political. It therefore lacks the grandeur seen in Tutaria and is more utilitarian in nature. It is home to the Emerald Quarter, the Ruby Quarter, the Amber Quarter, the Obsidian Quarter, the Topaz Quarter, and the Sapphire Quarter.

# THE TUTARIAN MOUNTAIN RANGE

The first and main territory of the Dwarves. Its beauty is beyond compare among the races and hosts the largest library in Chartile. It is home to the Amethyst Quarter, the Cobalt Quarter, the Moonstone Quarter, the Garnet Quarter, the Citrine Quarter, the Opal Quarter, the Carnelian Quarter, and the Diamond Quarter.

# THE EMERALD QUARTER

The area of Mount Kelsii designated for visiting guests such as Elven royalty and nobility, visiting Elders from Tutaria, visiting trainees from Tutaria, and various Ambassadors.

# THE SAPPHIRE QUARTER

A quarter within Mount Kelsii. The living quarters of Dwarvik royalty, current Elders, and where individuals in training for royalty live and study. On occasion, Elven nobility will reside here.

# THE CRYSTAL QUARTER

The Fortress center which includes meeting areas, the food ration distribution complex, religious temples, and military training centers and weapons store.

# THE HALL OF RASHIRI

Said to be the wonder of Mount Kelsii, the Hall of Rashiri is the main religious temple of the Dwarves in the mountain. Two of the four walls stand at the edge of the mountain's face and hold huge slabs of stained glass that catch the morning and afternoon light, casting a rainbow of colors throughout the chamber. The seats are arranged in a spiral, broken only by a single aisle leading from the main door to the altar at the very center.

# THE GREAT PASSAGE

Built in the time of the four kings, this tunnel extends under the Great Plains from Mount Kelsii to the foothills of the Tutarian Mountains. Sheltered from the elements above ground, a traveler can decrease their time between the Dwarvik strongholds considerably.

# THE GREAT PLAINS

Its original name has long since been lost, located in the flat expanse between Mount Kelsii and Tutaria, and the Wailing Cliffs and the Belirian Forest. It was the home of many Lost Legends that have since passed out of knowing. It was possibly the home of the Centaur clans. Now, it is used by Dwarvik and Elven shepherds.

# SWANSDALE, OHIO

Located in Fulton County, Swansdale is a small, rural community. Its population is so small, it is still considered a Village, and not even a Town.

# CRANBROOK ART ACADEMY

An elite school for the arts. A two-hour drive from Swansdale, Ohio. Attended by Jayson Hill's sister, Jessica Hill.

# FORT MEIGS

A United States Fortification built along the Maumee River during the War of 1812. Visted by Leo on a class field trip where he first heard of a combat defensive position known as The Plow.

# OTHER

## KING FLORINE

One of the last known Dwarvik male royals. Florine helped establish a script and system of writing that could be used between the races.

## KING JENEMAR

The King of the Elves who negotiated a temporary truce between the four kings and Duke Noraedin's army. It was Jenemar who suggested that if a settlement could not be made with Noraedin, that they would use the circlet to kill the Duke.

## KING KASMALIN

The last known Merfolk royal. Formally The Kas of Marlintole Spoke, and nicknamed Kasmalin by Jenemar as children. Little is known about Kasmalin. Many believed he was far more intelligent than his other fellow kings and had greater magical abilities. However, he chose not to use his magic very often and took a stance of neutrality most of the time. He was the only one of the four kings against the use of the circlet to kill Duke Noraedin. Kasmalin slowly faded into history. There is no known record of his death or where he went after the death of Noraedin.

# KING PASALPHATHE

The last king of the Human race. Elder brother to Duke Noraedin, known for his boisterous personality and hot temper. When Noraedin was overthrown and order brought to Chartile once more, Pasalphathe was eventually put into orenite cuffs and faded away into history.

# DUKE NORAEDIN

Brother of King Pasalphathe, and one of the most powerful wielders of magic within Chartile at the time. Noraedin was also a great alchemist. Some believed he poisoned his own parents to try at attain the throne. Noraedin was able to bring many elves (and humans) under his banner as the rightful king.

# BECK-ANDS

Short for Beck-And-Calls, the name given to Human slaves.

# KRISTA

Beck-and to the Lord of Cannondole.

# DUJ'ANAH

Mother of Dimitri. Secret lover to Nahiri. Human slave acquired by Empress Nefiri at the behest of her brother, Nahiri. Later elevated to the position of Head Retainer to the Empress, a position of great significance and previously always held by Dwarves, never by a Human.

# THE COUNCIL OF THE ELDERS

A group of individuals, each representing a different Quarter of either Mount Kelsii or The Tutarian Mountains. Each person is elected by those residing in each Quarter.

# THE CONCLAVE OF NOBLES

Each region within the Elven territory of Chartile is represented by a lord, duke, or baron. These individuals convene and meet to advise the Royals on matters of State. Though they hold no real power, the king and queen often defer to what the Conclave wishes to keep the peace.

# FIRON TUTOR

The *firon tutor* is an ancient Chartilian blade. It is thin and light weight and made popular by noble ladies. Over time, varying lengths of *firon tutors* were made, the longer of which became the popular choice for official duels. The shorter, and original lengths for the blades were worn by most noble ladies, and it became an art of hiding pockets in clothing in which the blade would fit and fashioning hilts that could be mistaken for jewelry.

The blade was inspired by the legend of *The Firon Uprising* in which the fourteen wives and fourteen daughters of fourteen cloth merchants turned on their cruel husbands and fathers by brandishing their spinning wheel spindles upon them.

# THE FIVE-DAY FEVER

An illness most commonly known for the fever that comes on quickly and lasts for an average of five days. Most cases result in death. There was a rampant outbreak of Five-Day Fever several years after Runa married Aramor. Because of Runa's distribution and teaching of medicine, the plague was more easily contained with fewer deaths.

# RIVER LUNG

Common among fisherman and sailors who lived in areas with dense and frequent fog. Manifesting with a wet cough deep in the lungs. Can be fatal to the elderly.

# THE ORACLE

A flat, highly polished piece of obsidian surrounded by running water. It is said to emit a pulsating vibration that connects one to Rashiri to receive her wisdom. Training is required to use the Oracle as the vibrations have been known to cause severe headaches, and even bleeding.

# THYRUNI'S JEWELS

Hard deposits resembling tiny gemstones formed inside the body and passed through the urine. Most common in male dwarves and first identified by a Dwarvik healer and physician named Thyruni. Many who suffer from the condition will wear the washed and polished stones on a necklace as a sign of bravery and determination.

# BIDDING DAY

Twice a year, once in the Spring in the month of Pasalvar during the Melt Moon and once in the Autumn in the month of Kasmaqar during the Hunter's Moon, nobles and royals will make the journey down the Great River, around the shore of the Never Ending Sea to Duneland to acquire new beck-ands.

In the larger towns and quarters within the Elven and Dwarvik territories, other Bidding Days are held where merchants or lesser nobles may buy and sell beck-ands among each other.

52

# THE WAILING CLIFFS

A massive expanse of miles-high cliffs that run the length of Chartile from the Bay of Tal Isk'jabar to The Deep of Tomorrow in the ancient Merfolk Kingdom. Named for sound made by the constant wind that sounded as if a thousand souls were screaming or wailing. After the Great War had ended, the many magical creatures of Chartile disappeared behind the towering walls of the Wailing Cliffs. Anyone who dared to scale them was never heard from again.

# DESERT GLASS

Different from other types of man-made glass, desert glass is completely transparent. It is seen most commonly when lightning strikes the sand at high temperatures, however, history has recorded instances where an individual was able to create small pieces of desert glass with magic.

# HISTORIES, LORE, AND TALES

*In a place before anything was,*
*and nothing was only a thought,*
*when time and space collided,*
*here is where magic was wrought.*

*From the darkness crept forth into light,*
*and from the light the night time was made,*
*The Creator brought forth into being,*
*five creatures Its bidding to aid*

*With feathers as blue as the sky,*
*and talons as strong as the stone,*
*what we now know and call The Gryffin,*
*made the mountains and land its own.*

*At dawn it unfurled its wings,*
*and shook forth the dew of the night,*
*and here fell the gems of the mountains,*
*with dazzling colors and might.*

*And by the magic and will of the land,*
*by the strength and foundations of ore,*
*the first of the dwarves were made here,*
*from the gems these people were born.*

Chartile Creation Myth, Part 1

# THE INCIDENT AT OUTLAND POST

In the spring of Piper's fourteenth year, Elven soldiers came to Outland Post. They claimed to be recruiting for the King's army, though 'forcing' would have been a better word. Whisperings of a rogue organization were taking root among the Eleven territories. King Aramor was often gravely ill, and his daughter, Princess Taraniz, had stepped willingly into the role of commander. Her knowledge and leadership qualities were both surprising and rather terrifying. Taraniz was determined to take out any criminal establishment.

Piper, however, stood her ground against these soldiers and tried to save the children far too young for such bloodshed. Having studied the laws of her kingdom, she knew the elves outlawed conscription. But her defiance only enraged the soldiers and fueled the villagers into further anger and rebellion.

When Nevan saw the magic sparking around his daughter's clenched fists, he ordered Paria to take her home. This only angered Piper more. She felt she should be there fighting alongside her neighbors and friends as it was she who had started it all. Piper used her magic to light the kitchen heart, but in her anger, she could not control it. She tried to use her magic again to keep the fire from spreading, but this only created more.

In the end, dozens of villagers and soldiers were dead, including several of the children Piper had grown up with, and her own parents. Fearing retribution from the soldiers, she fled to the foothills of Mount Kelsii. The soldiers dispatched messenger birds to the palace from a larger town along the river as they awaited further orders.

Princess Taraniz herself arrived at the village with an armed guard, ready to take Piper into custody. It was Valar, disguised as one of the princess's guards, that persuaded Taraniz to instead cast Piper into the wilds. Citing concerns that she may destroy the entire Belirian Forest on their way back to the palace was enough to convince the deranged princess. It was this act of kindness that allowed Kaytah to continue caring for her granddaughter in secret from a distance.

# THE NOBLE DEEDS OF LADY RUNA VOUCLAINE

The town of Harpy's Pointee lay close to The Neverending Sea. This made it an ideal environment for growing many of the herbs needed for medicines.

When she was sixteen, Runa accompanied her father and brother on several weeks-long treks during the tournament season. Though it was highly suspected she would wed Valar, Lord Raoul wanted options. Not only for himself, but for his daughter. She had seen little of the world beyond the Barony of Lochtir, and he hoped she might fall for a young noble at the tournaments.

But that was not what drew Runa's attention. Instead, she saw first-hand the need for the unique medicinal herbs customary to the barony outside its borders. During the next year's tournament season, she distributed the herbs and medicines to every village and town she could travel to while her father and brother competed. News of her endeavors quickly spread. Healers from smaller villages came to the larger towns and cities to learn from her. She taught them how to use the herbs, and how to grow them outside of their ideal climate of Harpy's Pointee.

Upon returning home, Runa asked her mother to commission the Conclave for more roadways to the main road along the Great River that led to Harpy's Pointee. This would allow quicker access to the fresh and stored herbs during times of illness and increase other trade routes. Lady Odette, however, insisted her daughter commission the Conclave herself.

With Valar at her side for support, Runa's petition to the Conclave was so strong, it was not only accepted, it earned her additional fame and recognition across the kingdom.

Queen Eleanor was not blind to these great deeds, even before Runa's address to the Conclave. She arranged the marriage between Runa and Aramor when Runa was nineteen - just before Valar intended to propose to her.


# THE PRINCESS AND THE KNAVE

Teaching Isla the effects of dreamshade tea was probably one of the best and worst things the Elders could have done. As elder Tyrna slept, Isla carefully crept into the darkness of the Sapphire Quarter beyond. The little bells she had wrapped tightly in her pocket jingled quietly, and she prayed to Rashiri no one would notice.

The eastern mines had long since dried up of any usable orenite. But it hadn't kept the dwarves from digging deeper and trying to find another pocket hidden beneath the granite and limestone. It was only after three cave-ins were the mines shut down and evacuated.

No one had visited them since – except Isla.

A guard on patrol rounded a corner ahead, and Isla quickly ducked into the shadows. If anyone knew, she might forfeit her training as Princess. She would return to her family disgraced. She held her breath as the guard passed and waited for him to disappear into the darkness. She quickened her pace and hurried toward the eastern tunnels. She squeezed through the barricade, careful not to rip her dress as she had done once before. Explaining that to elder Tyrna had not been easy. But they could never know.

"Brande! Brande!" Kylani called, not caring to keep his voice down. The nocturnal singing frogs in the boughs of the Belirian trees were the only reply.

It had been over a week since Brande had disappeared. The boy was too stubborn for his own good. His acceptance into the soldier program had been denied, leaving him heartbroken and seemingly without a purpose. Brande had studied for his entire youth expecting to be recruited like their older brothers. Two inches had stood between him and his passion. Two inches of height more, and he would have been accepted.

The night air was growing colder, and Kylani was sure Brande wasn't in the area. He stepped away from the forest line and looked up at the silhouette of the mountain before him. It was almost impossible to see the path that led around to the southern entrance. Hidden behind a mess of flowering gryffin vines, Kylani saw the glint of a jewel. He climbed the precipice before him and brushed aside the bright, blue petals that had begun to bloom. The outline of a door stood before him. It was marked with a familiar hematite stone indicating the entrance to a mine. Another gust of wind brushed against his skin. He shivered and pushed the door open.

The bell-covered ankle bands had taken Isla months to make in secret. The leather strap had been easy to come by, but the bells had been the most difficult. She worked by candlelight beneath her pillow to muffle the sound. Now, she could finally practice the traditional wedding dance of the dwarves.

She removed her cloak and set it on an abandoned cart that was still attached to the old rail system. The cavern was massive, and the bells echoed off the tall ceilings as she walked. It sounded exactly like the weddings she attended in the Crystal Quarter.

Step. Step. One, two three. Step. Step. Three, two, one, and skip. Isla heard the music that would have accompanied the wedding dance in her mind. Step. Step. One, two, "Dang it!" She sighed and started the music in her mind over again.

Dwarvik law forbade her from ever taking a husband now that she was in training as a royal. She would never know the Dance of the Bells or the taste of ginger cake. But she could have this. This private moment to dance to the darkness, the only husband she would ever know.

Kylani shut the door quietly behind him and was immediately plunged into darkness. The sound of bells echoed in the wide chamber, and he stopped short.

"Step. Step. One, two, three," he heard a soft voice whisper.

"Hello?" Kylani asked.

The bells stopped.

"Hello?" Kylani asked again, stepping forward in the dark. "Is someone there?"

He heard the bells again, closer this time, but much quieter. He ran forward and slammed into the side of an empty rail cart.

Someone screamed, and Kylani fell to the floor, trying to catch the breath that had been knocked from his lungs.

"Wait!" he coughed. "I'm not going to hurt you. Gah!" He couldn't move his left arm.

"Are you hurt?" a gentle voice asked.

In the darkness, Kylani felt someone kneel beside him, and a hand found its way to his shoulder. It wasn't the rough skin of the healers he had trained under. It was soft and made his skin tremble.

"I – I think I–" The hand touched his arm and he cried in pain.

"I'm sorry! Here, let me help you." She reached under his arm and pulled him to his feet with surprising strength. "Come, follow me."

"How–" The mine was still pitch black. Kylani reached out with his good arm and felt for the mine cart he had run into.

"I've come here for weeks. I know the way." The soft hand rested Kylani's palm on her shoulder. "Follow me."

One step at a time, Kylani followed the sound of the bells through the darkness, then watched the outline of a door emerge before him. They exited into the empty corridor outside the abandoned orenite mines.

Thank yo–" Kylani turned and stared open-mouthed at Isla of Arnkatla, the future Princess of Tutaria.

She knelt and quickly removed a pair of wedding bell ankle bands, pulling a cloth from the pocket of her cloak, and wrapping the bands before shoving them in her pocket once more.

"What are you doing here?" Kylani asked.

Isla looked up and immediately felt her cheeks flush. She wished they were still shrouded in darkness. The young man who looked down at her made her stomach dance uncontrollably.

"I – I," she stammered, still staring from where she knelt on the ground. Kylani held a hand out to her. She took it, fingers trembling, and he pulled her to her feet. "I came here to dance," she whispered.

Kylani smiled at her, his dark eyes glinting in the dim torchlight from the corridor beyond.

"I love dancing," he said.


## HISTORY OF THE HAREBELL INN

In 1887, Thomas Foster, a well-to-do printing and publication merchant from

Boston, Massachusetts, purchased a piece of land in the seaside town of Cambden (later renamed Camden after it's split with Rockport several years later), in Maine.

At the time, Boston was a hot spot for literary movements, and Foster wished to garner favor with those influencers that held the ear of writers and journalists of the time. To which end, he constructed a residence in the Second Empire style, firstly as a summer home for his large family, but also as a retreat for prominent guests.

By 1890, his wife, Martha, spent much of her time tending to the needs of Thomas's guests at their Cambden home alongside her two daughters. Thomas's son, James, worked in Boston with his father, practicing his own socialite skills and managing the printing press.

On November 10th, 1892, a fire erupted in the basement of the Cleveland Store (later Village Shop). So great was its ferocity, that it climbed up the elevator shaft and burst out the roof, quickly spreading to the surrounding buildings of Main Street, Elm Street and Washington Street.

The water pressure from the fire department soon gave out, and a strong easterly wind spread the fire until over forty buildings in the business district were desecrated to little more than ash and rubble.

Though Foster's residence was spared, it was only just. The western side of the house was covered in soot, and the ground was scorched clean.

While Thomas and James came together with other businessmen in Camden (newly named since it's split from Rockport) to rebuild the business district, Martha and her daughters, Alice and Minnie, opened their home to the surrounding residents who had nowhere else to go.

In the spring of 1893, most of the new buildings in Camden had been rebuilt, including a new printing house managed exclusively by Thomas, who had given his Boston location over to James. Now, Thomas, Martha, Alice, Minnie, and Minnie's husband, John, lived in the Camden residence.

It was April when the first blossom was found poking through a thin frost on the western side of the house. Nothing had grown there since the fire, but there they were, tiny harebell flowers found by young Alice. It was this that gave the Fosters a new hope and inspiration, and the Harebell Inn was founded thus.

# THE TAKING OF PASALPHATHE

The Wailing Cliffs were always dark. High and towering, their shadows spread wide like a black blanket across the sands of Nazarakapi. The wind whipped fiercely, as it always did, echoing in the great expanse and tricking anyone who had never experienced their gales that a thousand angry souls were screaming their laments to the Creator. Against the backdrop of early morning, a troupe of figures congregated across the dunes, heading toward the entrance of a small cave.

The four kings of Chartile awoke only a few days prior with the same message ringing in their minds, a message of a possible truce with the man who had torn their worlds apart. As they approached the entrance that had been given to them in flashes of images as they slept, they could feel the tension rising in the air. The centaurs stomped nervously and gripped the hilts of their swords. The qarveenas' wings quivered in anticipation. They were warned not to join their minds to anyone or anything during this meeting, a feat not so easily achieved for their species.

A dark-haired man rested a hand on the smallest qarveena's back, and she turned her golden eyes to him.

"Stay here," he said. "There's no need to put you all in danger."

"Pasalphathe," said another man above the wailing gusts, "we're not leaving you."

"A Cast of Many Lights is right," said one centaur. "My king, this could very well be a trap."

A large dark man descended from his gryffin mount and adjusted the sword hanging from his belt. "You didn't really think we'd let you walk in there by yourself, did you?" he asked, the glint in his eye like the sun on precious gems.

"He is my brother," said Pasalphathe.

"Yes, and he is also the greatest threat to all the races in Chartile," the thin form of Jenemar replied. He raised an eyebrow at Pasalphathe. "There's no way to know what threats await us in there."

"Pasalphathe," said A Cast of Many Lights again, "We cannot deny Noraedin's magic is the greatest Chartile has ever seen. It also means it's the most dangerous."

"Which is why I can't risk something happening to you. It would not do to have the four kings of Chartile killed at once when my brother desires to become the king of *all* of Chartile. We'd be playing right into his hands."

"Then let the kings' guards accompany them!" said the sarangay commander, a small tendril of smoke curling from its nose.

The battalion nodded in agreement, and Chartile's four kings marched through the cave entrance, flanked by their personal guards. The darkness of the tunnel seemed to devour what little light found its way in from the mouth of the cave. Jenemar fashioned an orb of red light in the palm of his hand, and Florine followed suit, holding it aloft to light the way. Talons and hooves and the hard tread of boots echoed off the surrounding stone as they walked deeper into the cave.

Jenemar watched A Cast of Many Lights tense before him. He squeezed the man's shoulder. "All right, Kasmalin?" he asked, using the childhood nickname he had given to the King of the Merfolk years ago.

Kasmalin nodded. "Small spaces," he mumbled, and Jenemar gave him a sympathetic nod before returning to silence once more.

The tunnel turned sharply, and as they rounded the corner, a faint blue light shone up ahead. The centaur lifted his sword in its scabbard, but Pasalphathe caught his eye. He shook his head, the light from Jenemar's red orb making the Human's golden skin appear as if it were made of fire.

Florine paused suddenly, holding his orb up to the walls. Condensation rolled down the glistening black stone, and he placed his free hand against the rock face. It was smooth.

"What is it?" the sarangay asked.

"Desert glass," Florine whispered.

Pasalphathe paused as well. "Desert glass? The amount of energy needed to…" The man trailed off.

"Why would someone do this?" Kasmalin asked.

"*How* is more the question," said Jenemar joining them and holding his own red orb aloft.

No one answered.

When the storms of the Harvest Moon converged on the Nazarakapi desert, lightning would on occasion strike the sands, creating what was known as desert glass. To cover the walls of the cavern in it would require immense energy. Though none dared say it, they all were thinking the same anxious thought. Their march through the tunnel was an intentional demonstration of Noraedin's power. The gryffin clicked its beak in agitation and fluffed its fur and feathers. Florine stroked the creature's neck, attempting to calm his friend.

"Welcome, kings of Chartile," a booming voice called to them from the end of the tunnel.

The blue light grew brighter as they shared a determined glance between them. The centaur griped the hilt of his sword, and this time Pasalphathe did not stop him. They stepped from the tunnel and into an enormous cavern that sparkled and glistened from the blue fire that danced gently around the perimeter. Before them sat a man upon a throne made of shining dessert glass. He smiled at them, spreading his arms wide in greeting. The group fanned out, hands twitching above their weapons. Even the gryffin remained tense, scraping its talons on the floor.

"Noraedin," said Pasalphathe, "Brother, why have you called us here?"

The shadows from the fire danced across Noraedin's terra-cotta skin. As Pasalphathe spoke, he saw movement along the edges of the cavern. Flashes of spears and swords from a dozen Humans surrounded the group. Pasalphathe's own people.

"To make a deal with you, Sal," said Noraedin, and his older brother cringed at the name.

Jenemar stepped forward, halting the sharp-tongued retort he knew was working it's way past Pasalphathe's lips.

"The Rule of Order has fallen," Jenemar said. "Our peoples are in chaos. Friends have turned to foes, sons against fathers–"

"And brothers against brothers?" Noraedin said coyly.

"My people are divided as well," said Florine. "More so than they have ever been. Many are refusing to work the mines at all, fearing the discovery of this orenite is the cause of everything."

Noraedin did not answer. He stared down at the kings, his dark eyes and vicious smile boring into their souls.

"Noraedin," said A Cast of Many Lights, "my people are turning from the path of light. They are killing themselves in droves. They cannot comprehend the darkness they now face."

Noraedin stood from his throne, signaling to his people to lower their weapons.

"This saddens me greatly," he said, "to hear of such devastation across my land. My heart aches at the thought of their suffering."

"Then end this, brother!" Pasalphathe implored.

"I *could* end this," Noraedin said. "*You* could end this. With one simple gesture."

The kings exchanged worried glances, and their guards shifted uncomfortably behind them.

"Bow to me," Noraedin said. "Acknowledge me as the rightful King of Chartile."

"There has never been one ruler of all the races," Florine said coldly.

"But there could be," Noraedin said, his voice still gentle. "The Creator has gifted me the strongest magic of any man or beast of Chartile. It was I who discovered the orenite, and I who discovered the secret to unlocking our minds from this stupor, this ignorance we have all been forced to live in."

"It is not ignorance that causes bliss, but perhaps our bliss has made us ignorant to the greater threats we never knew existed," said Pasalphathe, trying to match his brother's tone. "Join us, Noraedin, and we will find a way to destroy the orenite. Together we can save Chartile from this dark magic."

"Oh, I have no intention of destroying the orenite," said Noraedin, his eyes narrowing.

"Noraedin, what are you planning?" A Cast of Many Lights asked tentatively.

The Elven Duke ignored him. "I shall give you all one last chance." He squared his shoulders, towering over them as his lip threatened to curl in anger. "Bow before your king!"

"There is no King of Chartile, Noraedin," said Jenemar, squaring his own shoulders alongside his comrads. "And there never will be."

At once, the humans surrounding the group converged on them. A Cast of Many Lights raised his hands, calling to him the water that dripped from the glass walls. Florine drew his sword as his gryffin lunged forward to protect him.

Pasalphathe dove through the freezing drops of water and heard the wall of ice Kasmalin had created solidify behind him. He rushed the steps of the glass throne, his sword drawn and flaming with brilliant fire. Noraedin glared at him, raising his hand and lifting Pasalphathe from his feet.

"Pasalphathe!" Jenemar cried. He swung his bow staff, amplifying his cry of distress and sending its sound wave at three advancing humans. "Kasmalin, lower the wall!"

"There's too many!" Florine said as more humans emerged from the shadows. They were relentless, throwing magic more powerful than they had ever encountered. The sarangay gripped his shield with white-knuckled fingers, falling back to protect Kasmalin from the onslaught of magic. The strain caught in his throat with a guttural groan as he held off the magic, but barely.

Florine watched as one of their attackers snapped his spear in half. The dwarf furrowed his brow, wondering if this was a gesture of surrender. With a flick of his wrists, the broken spear became a set of ropes. They flew through the air, winding themselves around the gryffin's feet and pulling him to the ground. Florine rushed to his friend, cutting the ropes, and pushing the creature back down in time to avoid another encounter with this new, strange magic.

"We have to get out of here!" he cried.

Beyond the ice wall, Noraedin narrowed his eyes at Pasalphathe who dangled in the air before him.

"You should have bowed when you had the chance," he said, his magic tightening around Pasalphathe's throat.

"I'll–Never–" Pasalphathe spluttered, but with each breath, he felt his brother's magic growing stronger, and his own weakening. The edges of his vision grew dark, as the fire of his sword went out. He pulled in a last breath before his sword clattered to the floor, and he fell unconscious.

"Pasalphathe!" Jenemar called again. He beat against the ice wall Kasmalin held in place.

The sarangay pulled him back down the tunnel, Florine and the gryffin doing their best to hold back the growing throng of humans.

"We'll save him, Jenemar," said Kasmalin. He lowered his hands and the ice wall splintered into a thousand pieces showering over their enemy. "We'll find a way to get him back."

They emerged from the tunnel as a thundering met their ears. Kasmalin fell to his knees as the entrance to the tunnel crumbled and caved in with a shudder that shook the sands beneath their feet.

"What happened?" the centaur demanded as the qarveena flew across the sands to where they had collapsed.

The smallest qarveena stepped forward, gently pressing her forehead to Jenemar's. The man felt hot tears sting his eyes as he linked with the cat-like being, laying bear the events that had taken place moments ago.

She pulled back, offering the Elf King a nuzzle of sympathy before turning to the group. "They have taken Pasalphathe," she said.

## THE LEGEND OF THE FIRON UPRISING

Whilom and forever ago… there lived fourteen brothers. Fourteen brothers who lived in a crumbling castle they named Firon overlooking fourteen miles of green land on the edge of the sea. They grew the finest wool from their fourteen flocks of fourteen capricorn and spun the most beautiful cloth in all the land.

The fourteen brothers took fourteen brides and gifted them with fourteen spinning wheels. And as they appraised their fourteen flocks of fourteen capricorns, the fourteen brides, now fourteen wives, could hear them singing on the wind.

> *"Comb the fleece and wring and crease, till Phoenix light does flee,*
> *"Then spin anon on spindle long, and twist and draft and niddy-nod,*
> *"Thread the wefts until none left, or risk thy partners scorn bereft."*

Soon, the fourteen wives gave birth to fourteen daughters. All day long the fourteen mothers and fourteen daughters sat within the crumbling castled by the sea, spinning the most beautiful cloth in all the land from the finest capricorn wool.

The splendor of their creations spread far and wide across the land and across the sea. The fourteen brothers grew more and more wealthy, adorning their glorious garments with jewels and sparkling metal threads. They wore their wealth with pride, until it turned to vanity, and all the while, they sang to their fourteen wives and fourteen daughters, the song of threat and torment.

> *"Comb the fleece and wring and crease, till Phoenix light does flee,*
> *"Then spin anon on spindle long, and twist and draft and niddy-nod,*

And though their fingers often bled, and the wool was stained from tears they shed, for years on end the fourteen wives and fourteen daughters spun and spun and spun the most beautiful cloth in all the land.

When one day the fourteen mothers and fourteen daughters tired of the torment and torture of the fourteen brothers. They filled the pockets of the fourteen men with the jewels and metal threads they used to adorn their clothing. And when the brothers stood upon the cliffs, overlooking their fourteen flocks of fourteen capricorns, the women broke the spindles from their wheels, and chased the brothers for fourteen miles over the edge of the cliffs by the sea.

Down, down, down the fourteen brothers fell until they tumbled into the sea. They called and flailed, grabbing for their fourteen flocks of fourteen capricorns. But their glorious garments, made from the most beautiful cloth, and spun from the finest wool in all the land were heavy with pride and vanity, and they sank deep into the sea, never to be seen again.

WINTER
SPRING
SUMMER
AUTUMN
DARK MOON
ICE MOON
MELT MOON
FLOOD MOON
SPIRIT MOON
SEED MOON
HUNTERS MOON
DRAKE MOON
HARVEST MOON
FIRE MOON
RHIDQAR
22 DAYS
MURENVAR
23 DAYS
PASALVAR
21 DAYS
TORHIRVAR
21 DAYS
PAVENQAR
21 DAYS
JENQAR
21 DAYS
KASMAQAR
21 DAYS
KAIQAR
21 DAYS
ANSALVAR
21 DAYS
FLORNVAR
21 DAYS

# ABOUT THE AUTHOR

CASSANDRA MORGAN was born in a small town in Ohio. She comes from a family of both writers and English majors from both sides of her family.

The idea for Chartile (pronounced KAR-tyl) came to Cassie when she was thirteen years old. It is loosely based on some of the games she and her friends would play.

Cassandra is a frequent guest at conventions and writing conferences in the Midwest area. She is a writing coach, a foster for orphaned kittens, and participates with The International Cat Association.

*Connect with Cassandra!*

WWW.AUTHORCASSANDRAMORGAN.COM
WWW.AUTHORCPMORGAN.COM

CONTACT@AUTHORCASSANDRAMORGAN.COM

WWW.FACEBOOK.COM/AUTHOR.CASSANDRA.MORGAN
TWITTER: @AUTHORCASMORGAN
INSTAGRAM: @MORGAN_CASSANDRA

www.ingramcontent.com/pod-product-compliance
Lightning Source LLC
Chambersburg PA
CBHW051235210726
48290CB00003B/969